Erotic Endeavors

Graciela Berry

HerLife HerWrite Publishing Co. LLC

ISBN: 978-1-7349232-8-5

Dedication

Dedication is to you, Graciela, because for years you have put other's needs and wants ahead of your own dreams. And finally, you did something you have been dreaming about since you were fifteen years old. I am so proud of you. The mother, the friend, the sister, the woman, who you have become, amazes me every day. Keep striving to be better than you were yesterday.

I love you, Boo.

Jasmine Ruth, SoJazzy Photography

Acknowledgement

God

My journey

Dreams

As she lays there in the room, she hears the wind blowing against her window. She hears the sirens of ambulances. She hears his voice whisper in her ear. She instantly gets cold. She pulls the covers over her body. He slowly begins to pull the covers off. He wanted to see how hard her nipples get when she is cold. He slowly begins to caress her breast. Flicking her, now, hard nipples. She looks into his eyes with timid and desperation. He places her breast in his mouth and she begins to moan in excitement. He slowly lies on top of her. Their naked bodies pressed up against each other. So many thoughts running through her head... He slowly caresses her hair away from her face, and then kisses her on her cheek, then down to her lips. She quivers with anticipation. Her skin racked with goose bumps. He then began to lick and kiss her neck. Then he grabbed her breast, nibbling on both at the same time. He loved to hear her moan and to see her facial expressions. He makes his way down to her abdomen with slow soft kisses. He reaches for her pussy, he looks up at her, and she's biting her bottom lip. He kisses her lips then her clitoris. He opens her up and kisses her inside. He places his tongue inside her, going in and out. She starts to move back. He pulls her by her hips bringing her closer to his mouth. She begins to grind her hips to match his tongue strokes. She grabs his head not wanting him to stop. He is licking all her juices not missing a drop. He places his fingers inside her, while his tongue is sucking on her clit. She moans and enjoys every moment. She looks down intoxicated by his tongue inside her. She felt like, she was in a different place. He reached new heights like never before. She screams out in ecstasy. She cums all in his mouth and he just ate it up. He places his fingers in and out some more and plays with her clit. She screams out again. Then she hears her alarms clock goes off, she sits up in the bed, and looks around no one is there. Her legs and sheets are soaked. She gets out of bed with distain. It's time for her to go to work now. She hates when she has vivid dreams...

Jerry Moore, Moore Photography

Remember

He started to reminisce about how her lips felt on his cheek. He started to think how they would feel on other parts of his body. He began to get hard as the thought of her lips wrapped around his dick. Wondering why she only kissed him on the cheek. She was a sophisticated and sexy woman. He just couldn't stop thinking of all the nasty things he wanted to do to her. He wished he could place his dick inside her and sleep there. Just so he can feel her pussy pulsating around him at all times. She felt that good.

Jerry Moore, Moore Photography

Meeting

So, I am sipping tea at our morning meeting, my mind racing, as always. The secretary is up talking about a bunch of nonsense. What am I cooking for dinner? Did I let the dog out this morning?

I was startled out of my thoughts when doors opened up and immediately the room goes silent. Not because he's the boss, but all the ladies are drooling over, Mr. Johnson. He then says, "Good Morning" to everyone. All I could do was smile. He starts going over this month's projects and how last month according to him, was "piss poor." I don't think he realizes how hard we work, but damn it! if he doesn't look good in his blue suit today. He ended all meetings like he did all the time, with a joke.

I wonder if he evens notices me, if he even knows who I am. Every time he slams his notebook on the desk, I imagine he's smacking my ass. It's something about a man in power that turns me on. I began to day dream about his dick inside of me imagining his strong hands all over my body. He is caressing my soft brown skin. My pussy began to get wet just thinking about it...I looked up and the meeting was over.

Jerry Moore, Moore Photography

Lost

Her legs stretched out,

His palms wrapped around her hips

Her body clings to his,

His breathing is calm

She feels his pace as their bodies embrace,

paralyzed by pleasure encapsulated forever

Jasmine Ruth, SoJazzy Photography

Oral Exam

I sit and imagine my lips around your dick going, up and down. I'm licking and sucking your dick while your tongue buried deep in my pussy. The sound of me moaning on your dick with the vibrations making you harder and harder, me massaging your balls, I place them in my mouth while still stroking your dick. I go back to your dick and take it all in and gag on it. You let out a moan. I plant my pussy right in position. You begin licking all my juices as they run down my thighs and onto your face drizzling onto your beard. I am still sucking your dick with intense pleasure, enjoying every moan you let out. Until, finally your dick releases your sweet cum into my mouth. I slurp it all up leaving nothing left. We finished our first test, but we are far from completing the course.

Jasmine Ruth, SoJazzy Photography

Him

As they lay there in the bed in silence, he smiles because he's happy he found her. She smiles because of him. His smile... His touch... His body... His vibe... His energy... She likes it all, better yet, she love it.

He lays there in awe of the events of the day. Today was the day to show him, it's him and only him. I sent chills down his spine, as my lips traced his body, loving on every inch of his body. Please Sir, just lay back and enjoy as I take control. As I allow my actions to speak louder than my words. Slow kisses on his brown skin. Enjoy his body reaction to my soft lips touching him. That skin on skin contact. He just lays back and enjoys the ride. My hands warm from the oils slowly began to caress and massage his body. Damn, the sight of the oil on his brown skin makes me wetter, than before. He slowly begins to get harder and harder as my hands follow my lips down to his penis. I grab the oil and pour it on his brown dick. I slowly begin to caress his beautiful dick, licking my lips because I want to take it all in my mouth. "Be patient," I tell myself.

I continue to caress the oil down his thighs and down to his feet. Making sure every inch of his beautiful brown skin gets loved on. I ask him to turn over. I straddle him from behind massaging his shoulders and back kissing his body. Admiring his glistening skin, I turn him back over and began to rub his dick. Watching it get harder and harder. I slowly begin to take him all in my mouth. Enjoying the taste of him and coconut oil, he let out a moan that excites me. I begin to lick and suck his dick while massaging his balls. He lets out a loud moan as he begins to fill my mouth. He looks down, as I look up at him,

saying..."Damn!"

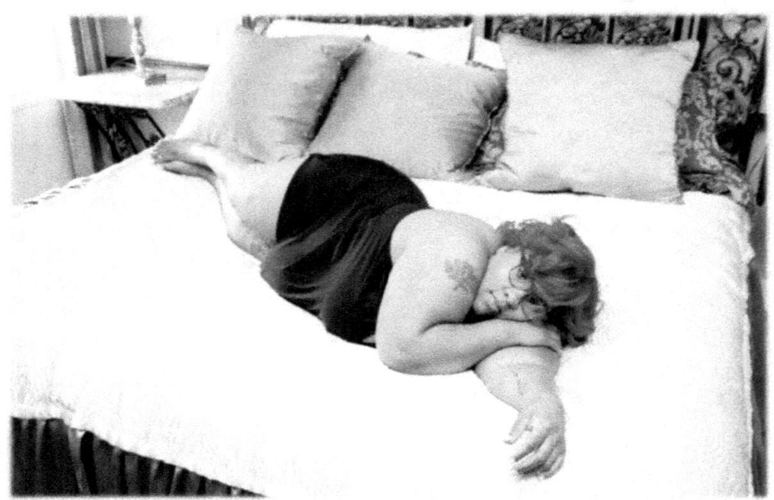

Jerry Moore, Moore Photography

Vibe

Let's Vibe...

Let me lay between your heart & mind

Let me explore your deepest secrets

I don't want to go in blind

Let me explore your soul

I want your story...

The one untold

Let's vibe…

Let me lay between your heart & mind

Let me try to find

Those broken pieces

Left behind

I want to help bind them

With my love defined

Let me lay between your heart & mind

Let me penetrate your thoughts

The ones you try to push away

Baby, I am not going anywhere

I am here to stay

Let me lay between your heart & mind

Let me swim in your ocean

I want to dive deep

Let's take this leap

Who knows where it'll lead

But for now baby...

Let's vibe...

Let me lay between your heart & mind

I promise to be kind

Jasmine Ruth, SoJazzy Photography

Run

She runs through his mine like the track he loves dearly. The track has never failed him. Feet hitting the pavement, sweat dripping down from his brow, mile after mile he conquers, just like he would like to conquer her. Sweat dripping, mind racing with thoughts of him deep inside her. Hearing her voice moan his name, he keeps running along the track with his thoughts racing faster than he is. Thinking about how deep he can go inside her. How she would look when he goes slowly at first, and then faster in and out of her. How great it would feel to cum inside her. How great it would feel for her to cum on his dick.

As he's running his dick is getting harder and harder as his body feels with anticipation for her. Sweat dripping down his neck, mind racing with thoughts of her riding his dick. How her pussy feels good wrapped around his dick? Sounds of his feet hitting the pavement, reminds him of the sound of her backing her ass into him when he's hitting it from the back. His mind is just enthralled in the feeling of her, until his phone lets out a ring telling him he has completed his course. He looks and notices his dick is hard. He walks over to his vehicle and jumps inside. He grabs his towel and wipes the sweat from his face and neck. All the while thinking, what is she doing right now? Should he call her? Should he invite her over? He starts up his car and heads home.

Once he gets home he hops in the shower. Imagining it's her lips and hands all over his body. Water and soap suds dripping from his body. His thoughts begin to wonder again. How would it feel to taste her pussy? Is it as sweet as her personality? Is it as warm as her touch? Fuck it! He has made up his mind, he is calling her. He hops out of the shower, wraps a towel around him and heads to his room where his phone is. As he picks up his phone, he hears his doorbell rings. He wasn't expecting anyone. Still with only a towel wrapped around him he answers the door, it's her, with surprise and now with a hard dick.

He adjusts his towel to try to hide his erection. He then says, "Hey, lady! She says, "Hey, I was in the neighborhood wondering if you wanted company, but I see you're busy" pointing out his towel and wet body. He quickly says, "No! I just finished taking my shower after my daily run!" He then, invites her in. She thinks, finally! As she walks passed him, she could see he had an erection. She smiles a little knowing it's because of her. Her juices were already flowing from seeing his body when he opened the door. He does something to her body that she hasn't yet figured out what or even why. She caught him at the right time, she thought. She had been at work all day thinking about his hands all over her body. Wondering how he felt inside of her. How she would feel riding his dick? How he tasted in her mouth? She wanted him bad.

He then excused himself to the back room where he throws on some underwear, shorts, and a t-shirt. He comes back into the living room to find her on the couch with nothing on, but a black lace thong and black bra. Shocked, he just looks at her body in astonishment. It's everything he wanted and needed. Her body was like the best hills and valleys he's ever seen and he was ready to explore them. Wasting no time, he grabs her and lays her down on the couch and starts kissing her body. She lets out soft moans. His lips on her skin felt so soft and smooth. He begins to get harder than before, this is what he wanted all day. She feels her body flowing with juices. She has been thinking about him all day as well.

As he kisses her body his hands followed, grabbing her all over. Caressing her succulent breasts and putting them in his mouth enjoying the sweet nectar of them. He gets down to her pussy. He just looks at it like it's a piece of art. He opens her legs as far as she would let them go. He slowly starts kissing her inner thighs, her calves, then feet, and back up. Once he gets back to her pussy, he softly kisses her clit and her lips. He then opens her lips and kisses them. She is letting out soft moans, enjoying him pleasuring her. His lips on her lips feel so soft. He opens up her pussy lips and lets out a little moan enjoying the beauty of her pussy. He then takes her all in his mouth enjoying every last drop of her. She lets out a moan or two in enjoyment. He begins to lick all in and around her pussy and playing with her clit. His tongue feels better than she imagined. He’s just elated her pussy tastes as sweet as apple pie. He couldn’t get enough. She moans louder and louder until all her juices came flowing down and to her surprise, her drank it all up. He loved the taste of her juices, sweet like honey, as he licks all around until it’s gone.

He stands up only to be met by her mouth, ready to be wrapped around his dick. His head immediately went back as her warm lips collided with his hard dick. He could not have imagined how good her mouth feels around him. He does not want this experience to end. She opened her mouth and begins to go up and down on his dick. Licking and sucking all over him. He let several moans out while looking down at her. He begins to think about how her pussy must feel if her mouth feels this amazing. She is licking and sucking like it's her favorite popsicle. He tastes so good to her, sweet and tart like pineapples. She begins to massage his balls as she is sucking his dick. He lets out a loud moan and places his head back in pure ecstasy. She doesn't stop, enjoying the sound of his voice until his sweet release goes into her mouth. He looks down at her only to see her catching every drip from him sucking him dry like the Sahara Desert. She begins to think he taste better than she could've imagined. She looks up at him and all they both can do is smile.

She grabs him and lays him down. She begins to kiss his neck, down to his chest. Her kisses are followed by her soft hands trailing across his body. She begins to massage his penis, kissing the tip. His penis starts to get hard again. Just what she wanted and needed. He doesn't know what it is about her, but his body craves her. She gets up and just looks at his body laying there. She is just admiring his hard dick. It looks so beautiful to her. She climbs on top and places him inside her. Both let out a moan, and their strides matched each other so elegantly. He couldn't believe how amazing her walls feels around his dick. She begins to ride him like a horse she had when she was little girl. He began to grab her ass, then up to her shoulders to go deeper inside her. Her head went back in pure enjoyment. His dick felt so good inside her. She begins to slow down and he was not having it. He grabbed her and flipped her over entering her from behind. He looks down to see her beautiful ass as he began to make love to her. She then lets out a loud moan enjoying every inch of him.

Jasmine Ruth, SoJazzy Photography

Room 418

She's on the elevator headed to the 4th floor. Purse in hand, she takes her pocket mirror out and checks her lipstick. The elevator doors open, she heads down the hall to room 418. She knocked on the door. He opened the door with no hesitation. She walks in and he says, "Hello beautiful." She turns and says,"Hey you!" He closes the door and grabs her by the shoulder and kisses her. Enjoying the taste of her sweet lips, she slowly pulls away and begins to walk toward the open room. She drops her purse down on the table. He grabs her and pulls her to the bed taking off her clothes. He begins to kiss her neck, breast, down to her stomach then he pushes her down pulling her panties off. He licks his lips then begins to admire her pussy. His licks begin to devour her pussy like no man ever has. She moans out in pleasure. He lets out a moan enjoying how she tastes. She places her hands upon his head rubbing his hair, enjoying every tongue stroke every lick her body gets from him.

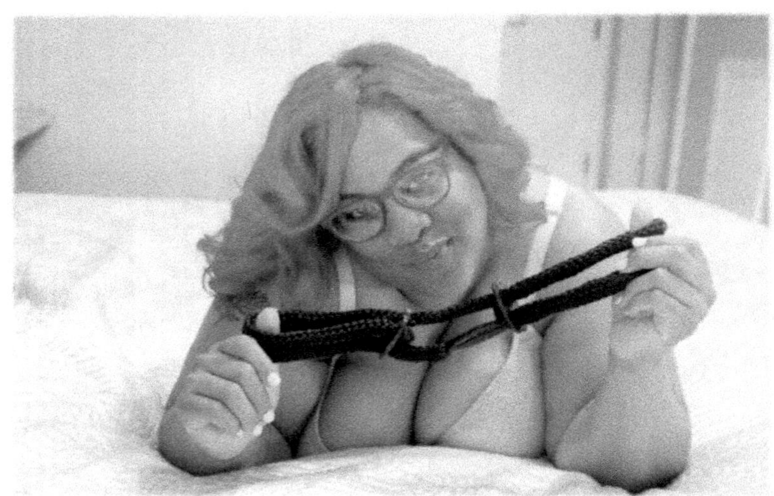

Jerry Moore, Moore Photography

Search

Love is…

Literally the thing that

Others crave for

Visibly pursuing what's believed to be

Everlasting,

but I search for

Happiness so I can be

Adored and

Pleased in every way not

Physical, but with real

Intimacy

Nurturing kind of happiness that

Evolves over time, when you can feel it in your

Spirit and

Soul, that soul happiness is spiritual healing

Thoughts

There is a clean crisp in the air. We both lay in anticipation of the others next move. Thoughts are just traveling a mile a minute. The things I want to do to you. The things I want you to do to me. Oh, how my body is yearning for your touch, your kiss, your manhood! I lean over and placed a kiss on your lips....hoping my little gesture was a hint! You kissed me back with such firmness. I began to run my fingers through your hair, around your face, down your neck, then to your chest all the while wondering if you want me as much as I want you. I begin to stroke your penis then with the slightest touch caress your inner thigh then up to your balls, watching you squirm with excitement. My hand slowly stroking your penis and rubbing the tip ever so lightly, I begin to feel you grow inside my hand. Oh, the thoughts of how good you would feel inside my mouth and inside of me, it begins to make my juices start flowing with excitement. I begin to slowly lick and suck the tip just to have a little taste! Ah, how good you taste to me. I slowly begin to move my mouth all the way down your penis filling my mouth up until it reached my throat! I then look up at you with such lust in my eyes, words fail you. You just bite your lip! I start to go up and down all on your penis, all the while lightly rubbing on your balls!

Thank You

Jasmine Ruth, SoJazzy Photography

www.ingramcontent.com/pod-product-compliance
Lightning Source LLC
LaVergne TN
LVHW020312110826
845148LV00017BA/2643

9781734923285